nickelodeon

BE BRAVE, LITTLE PUP

By Elle Stephens
Based on the screenplay by Billy Frolick and Cal Brunker & Bob Barlen
Based on the story by Billy Frolick
Illustrated by Fabrizio Petrossi

 A GOLDEN BOOK • NEW YORK

Published in the United States by Golden Books, an imprint of Random House Children's Books, a division of Penguin Random House LLC, 1745 Broadway, New York, NY 10019, and in Canada by Penguin Random House Canada Limited, Toronto. Golden Books, A Golden Book, A Little Golden Book, the G colophon, and the distinctive gold spine are registered trademarks of Penguin Random House LLC.

T#: 830191

rhcbooks.com

ISBN 978-0-593-37374-3 (trade)

Printed in the United States of America

10 9 8 7 6 5 4 3 2 1

2021 Edition

Hi, I'm Chase! I'm a rescue pup, and I'm part of the most PAWsome team ever: the PAW Patrol!

We live in Adventure Bay and are always ready for a rescue mission, no matter how big or small. Ryder is our leader. He's also my best friend!

I love my job and my team. But I wasn't always this happy.

When I was a tiny puppy, I lived on the streets of Adventure City. It was full of big buildings and loud cars. I was cold, hungry, and scared.

One morning, I was the most scared I had ever been—and then Ryder rescued me!

He brought me home to Adventure Bay and took care of me. He knew I could be a brave rescue pup, so he made me part of the PAW Patrol team. He has always believed in me.

Thanks to Ryder, I've had many adventures. And I've made the best friends!

But one day, the PAW Patrol got called to Adventure City. There was a terrible new mayor, and everyone was in danger.

"Come on, pups. Pack your things!" said Ryder.

I was going back to the big city.

Adventure City was even bigger than I remembered. I felt like a scared puppy again.

On our first rescue mission, we had to stop the mayor's crazy fireworks show. I was so nervous that I got stuck, and Marshall had to save me.

I felt awful. I had disappointed my friends and put people in danger. I didn't think the big city was for me.

But Ryder disagreed. He had an idea.

He showed me the street where he had rescued me.

"You were the bravest pup I'd ever seen," said Ryder.

I couldn't believe he thought I was brave even then! I knew I wouldn't let him down.

Just then, a huge storm cloud appeared over Adventure City. The mayor was using a cloud catcher to make sure the weather was nice for the grand opening of his new skyscraper. But the cloud catcher was full, and a giant storm was about to hit the city!

I was ready to join the PAW Patrol for our biggest city adventure yet!

My friends and I raced through the city and got everyone to safety.

Ryder rescued the mayor—but then Ryder needed help! I wasn't afraid of the big city anymore. I had to save my friend.

I rescued Ryder, and the PAW Patrol rescued Adventure City. I love being part of such a PAWsome team!

"Pup, pup, hooray!"